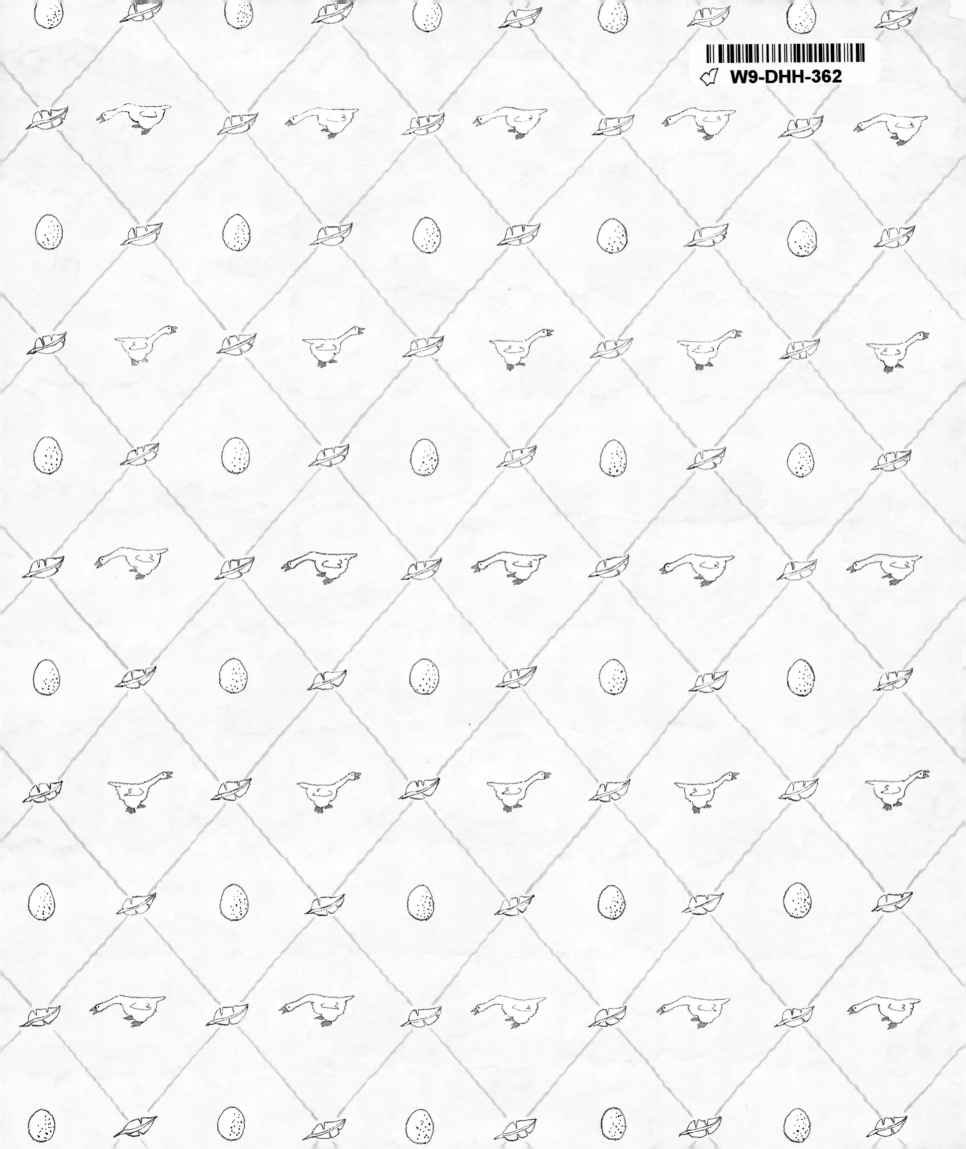

W9-DHH-362

For Debbie, Richard, Charles, and James

Magpie, magpie, flutter and flee; turn up your tail and good luck come to me.

KINGFISHER
Larousse Kingfisher Chambers Inc.
95 Madison Avenue
New York, New York 10016

First edition 1993
2 4 6 8 10 9 7 5 3 1

Copyright © Colin and Moira Maclean 1992

All rights reserved under Pan-American
and International Copyright Conventions

LIBRARY OF CONGRESS CATALOGING-IN-PUBLICATION DATA
Mother goose rhymes / illustrated by Colin & Moira Maclean.
1st American ed. p. cm.
Summary: includes over fifty favorite nursery rhymes
such as "Georgie Porgie," " Little Bo Peep," and "Three Blind Mice."
1. Nursery rhymes. 2. Children's poetry. [1. Nursery rhymes.]
I. Maclean, Colin, ill. II. Maclean, Moira, ill.
PZ8.3.M8525 1993
398.8 - dc20 92-26443 CIP AC

ISBN 0-7534-5155-7

Designed by Caroline Johnson
Printed in Spain

MotheR GoosE RhymeS

ILLUSTRATED BY

COLIN AND MOIRA MACLEAN

The cock doth crow to let you know if you be wise

Old Mother Goose,
When she wanted to wander,
Would ride through the air
On a very fine gander.

Mother Goose had a house,
'Twas built in a wood,
Where an owl at the door
For sentinel stood.

She had a son Jack,
A plain-looking lad,
He was not very good,
Nor yet very bad.

She sent him to market,
A live goose he bought;
See, mother, says he,
I have not been for nought.

'tis time to rise.

Jack's goose and her gander
Grew very fond;
They'd both eat together,
Or swim in the pond.

Jack found one fine morning,
As I have been told,
His goose had laid him
An egg of pure gold.

Jack ran to his mother
The news for to tell,
She called him a good boy,
And said it was well.

As I went over Lincoln Bridge, I met Mister Rusticap; pins and needles on his back,

To market, to market,
To buy a fat pig,
Home again, home again,
Jiggety-jig.

To market, to market,
To buy a fat hog,
Home again, home again,
Jiggety-jog.

Simple Simon met a pieman,
Going to the fair;
Said Simple Simon to the pieman,
Let me taste your ware.

Said the pieman to Simple Simon,
Show me first your penny;
Said Simple Simon to the pieman,
Indeed I have not any.

8

a-going to Thorney fair.

Tom, Tom,
　the piper's son,
Stole a pig
　and away he run;
The pig was eat,
And Tom was beat,
And Tom went howling
　down the street.

Cobbler, cobbler, mend my shoe,
Get it done by half-past two;
Stitch it up and stitch it down,
Then I'll give you half a crown.

Green cheese,
Yellow laces,
Up and down
The market places.

Smiling girls, rosy boys,
Come and buy my little toys;
Monkeys made of gingerbread,
And sugar horses painted red.

Ring-a-ring o' roses,
A pocket full of posies,
A-tishoo! A-tishoo!
We all fall down.

Three blind mice, see how they run!
They all ran after the farmer's wife,
Who cut off their tails with a carving knife,
Did you ever see such a thing in your life,
    As three blind mice?

in that? Now tell me if you can.

I'm the king of the castle,
Get down you dirty rascal.

Seesaw, Margery Daw,
Johnny shall have a new master;
He shall have but a penny a day,
Because he can't work any faster.

Here am I,
Little Jumping Joan;
When nobody's with me,
I'm all alone.

All work and no play makes Jack a dull boy; all play and no work makes Jack a mere toy.

A diller, a dollar,
A ten o'clock scholar,
What makes you come so soon?
You used to come at ten o'clock,
But now you come at noon.

Mary had a little lamb,
Its fleece was white as snow;
And everywhere that Mary went
The lamb was sure to go.

It followed her to school one day,
That was against the rule;
It made the children laugh and play
To see a lamb at school.

There was a little girl, and she had a little curl
Right in the middle of her forehead;
When she was good, she was very, very good,
But when she was bad she was horrid.

Here's Sulky Sue;
What shall we do?
Turn her face to the wall
Till she comes to.

And so the teacher turned it out,
But still it lingered near,
And waited patiently about
Till Mary did appear.

"Why does the lamb love Mary so?"
The eager children cry;
"Why, Mary loves the lamb, you know,"
The teacher did reply.

A, B, C, tumbledown D, the cat's in the cupboard and can't  see me.

A  A was an apple pie	**B**  B bit it	**C**  C cut it	**D**  D dealt it
E  E et it	**F**  F fought for it	**G**  G got it	**H**  H had it
I  I inspected it	**J**  J jumped for it	**K**  K kept it	**L**  L longed for it
M  M mourned for it	**N**  N nodded at it	**O**  O opened it	**P**  P peeped in it

Q quartered it

R ran for it

S sang for it

T took it

U upset it

V viewed it

W wanted it

XYZ and &
all wished for
a piece in hand.

One, two, three, four, five,
   Once I caught a fish alive;
Six, seven, eight, nine, ten,
   Then I threw it back again.

Why did you let it go?
   Because it bit my finger so.
Which finger did it bite?
   This little finger on the right.

Roses are red, violets are blue, sugar is sweet, and so are you.

Georgie Porgie, pudding and pie,
Kissed the girls and made them cry;
When the boys came out to play,
Georgie Porgie ran away.

Monday's child
is fair of face,

Tuesday's child
is full of grace,

Wednesday's child
is full of woe,

Thursday's child
has far to go,

High diddle ding, did you hear the bells ring?
The parliament soldiers are gone to the king.
Some they did laugh, and some they did cry,
To see the parliament soldiers go by.

Hippity-hop to the corner shop,
To buy a stick of candy,
One for you, and one for me,
And one for sister Mandy.

Lucy Locket lost her pocket,
Kitty Fisher found it;
Not a penny was there in it,
Only a ribbon round it.

Friday's child
is loving and giving,

Saturday's child
works hard for a living,

And the child that is born on the
Sabbath day
Is bonny and blithe, and good and gay.

March, march, head erect, left, right, that's correct.

Jack and Jill went up the hill,
To fetch a pail of water;
Jack fell down and broke his crown,
And Jill came tumbling after.

Then up Jack got, and home did trot,
As fast as he could caper;
To old Dame Dob, who patched his nob
With vinegar and brown paper.

Oh, the grand old Duke of York,
He had ten thousand men;
He marched them up to the top of the hill,
And he marched them down again.

And when they were up, they were up,
And when they were down, they were down,
And when they were only halfway up,
They were neither up nor down.

There was an old woman
Lived under a hill,
And if she's not gone,
She lives there still.

Four stiff-standers, four dilly-danders, two lookers, two crookers, and a wig-wag.

Little Boy Blue,
Come blow your horn,
The sheep's in the meadow,
The cow's in the corn.

Where is the boy
Who looks after the sheep?
He's under a haystack
Fast asleep.

Will you wake him?
No, not I,
For if I do,
He's sure to cry.

Baa, baa, black sheep,
Have you any wool?
Yes, sir, yes, sir,
Three bags full;

One for the master,
And one for the dame,
And one for the little boy
Who lives down the lane.

Lavender's blue, dilly, dilly,
Lavender's green;
When I am king, dilly, dilly,
You shall be queen.

Call up your men, dilly, dilly,
Set them to work,
Some to the plow, dilly, dilly,
Some to the cart.

Some to make hay, dilly, dilly,
Some to reap corn,
While you and I, dilly, dilly,
Keep ourselves warm.

Elsie Marley is grown so fine,
She won't get up to feed
     the swine,
But lies in bed till eight or nine.
Lazy Elsie Marley.

Little Bo Peep has lost her sheep,
And doesn't know where to find them;
Leave them alone, and they'll come home,
Bringing their tails behind them.

Davy Davy Dumpling, boil him in the pot; sugar him and butter him, and eat him

Polly put the kettle on,
Polly put the kettle on,
Polly put the kettle on,
We'll all have tea.

Sukey take it off again,
Sukey take it off again,
Sukey take it off again,
They've all gone
    away.

Little Poll Parrot
Sat in his garret
Eating toast and tea;
A little brown mouse
Jumped into the house,
And stole it all away.

Pease porridge hot,
Pease porridge cold,
Pease porridge in the pot
Nine days old.

Some like it hot,
Some like it cold,
Some like it in the pot
Nine days old.

Pat-a-cake, pat-a-cake, baker's man,
Bake me a cake as fast as you can;
Pat it and prick it and mark it with B,
Put it in the oven for baby and me.

Jack Sprat could eat no fat,
His wife could eat no lean,
And so between them both, you see,
They licked the platter clean.

while he's hot.

Little Miss Muffet
Sat on a tuffet,
Eating her curds and whey;
There came a big spider,
Who sat down beside her
And frightened Miss Muffet
    away.

Wash the dishes, wipe the dishes,
Ring the bell for tea;
Three good wishes, three good kisses,
I will give to thee.

Little Jack Horner
Sat in the corner,
Eating a Christmas pie;
He put in his thumb,
And pulled out a plum,
And said, "What a good boy am I!"

Down with the lambs, up with the lark; run to bed children before it gets dark.

Hush-a-bye, baby, on the tree top,
When the wind blows the cradle will rock;
When the bough breaks the cradle will fall,
Down will come baby, cradle, and all.

Wee Willie Winkie runs through the town,
Upstairs and downstairs in his nightgown,
Rapping at the window, crying through the lock,
Are the children all in bed, for now it's eight o'clock?

Cackle, cackle, Mother Goose,
Have you any feathers loose?
Truly have I, pretty fellow,
Half enough to fill a pillow.
Here are quills, take one or two,
And down to make a bed for you.

Bye, baby bunting,
Daddy's gone a-hunting,
Gone to get a rabbit skin
To wrap his baby bunting in.

Diddle, diddle, dumpling, my son John,
Went to bed with his trousers on;
One shoe off, and one shoe on,
Diddle, diddle, dumpling, my son John.

Hush-a-baa, baby,
Dinna mak' a din,
An' ye'll get a cakie
When the baker comes in.

Moon, moon, mak' me a pair o' shoon, and I'll dance till you be done.

Hey diddle, diddle,
The cat and the fiddle,
The cow jumped over the moon;
The little dog laughed
To see such sport,
And the dish ran away with the spoon.

Index of first lines

go to bed early, grow very tall.

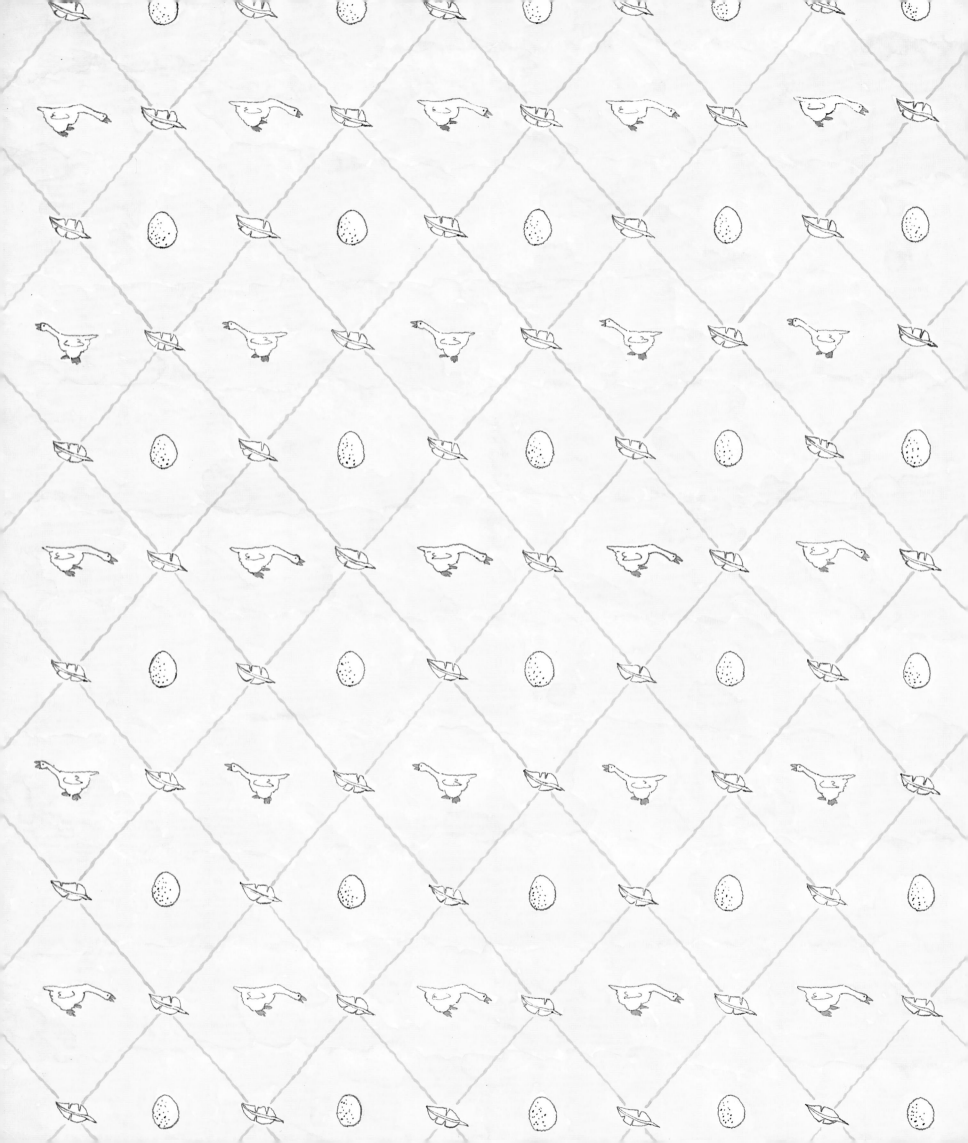